Jean Wright

As Light as Air

ISBN/EAN: 9783337123222

Printed in Europe, USA, Canada, Australia, Japan

Cover: Foto ©Andreas Hilbeck / pixelio.de

More available books at **www.hansebooks.com**

Jean Wright

As Light as Air

As Light as Air.

As Light as Air.

Verses by Jean Wright
Water color by Emma Keats Spe

FLEXNER & STAADEKER
Louisville, MDCCCXCII.

"YOUTH AND LOVE AND A SUMMER DAY."

ONE can not be a dying swan
                    Off hand—
One can't become a Raphael
                    On demand—
One can but do one's best—
                    And do no more—
So patience, Gentle Public,
                    We implore,
And bear in mind, we meekly beg of you,
                    Wise Buddha's rule—
          (I think its No. 2)
" Kill not—for pity's sake and lest you slay
  The meanest thing upon its upward way."

AS light as air the merry jest,
 Where all's in pantomime expressed—
  The crackling whip Ar'chino vaults to.
  Old Pantaloon all trembling halts to—
 Gay Harlequin, with knavish zest,
 His love for Columbine confessed.

   The lively tune that maidens waltz to.
   The pretty vows that lads are false to,
  The mellow laugh, the merry jest,
            Are light as air.

While motes dance on with half mad zest,
Low down, with passion half suppressed,
 Sings some poor wretch that life's been false to,
 The old refrain, that music halts to,
"Comme la vie est amere"—confessed,
La vie's a trifling thing at best—
          As light as air.

AH, truth to tell,
       'Tis sweet to lie
Within some fair and shady dell.
Ah, truth to tell,
'Tis sweet to yield to love's sweet spell—
       —I'll give him sigh for sigh—
For, truth to tell,
       'Tis sweet to lie.

THAT *nez retroussé*—'Tis a pity
  I make for subject of my ditty;
    Unsentimental choice—and yet—
    I pray, forgive if I forget
  To praise the points *you* think are pretty.

Ah, Love, would I were wise or witty!
  I'd send you something fine—and yet.
  Strive as I may, I can't forget
        That *nez retroussé*.

Ah, Phyllis dear, your hair is pretty,
Your eyes alone are worth a ditty,
  Your mouth with dainty pearls is set,
  Your *tout ensemble's* fair—and yet,
I will remember—more's the pity—
        That *nez retroussé*.

Marguerite.

WITH your dainty bit of sewing,
                    Marguerite,
And your smile, half shy, half knowing,
                    Wholly sweet,
And the rings of chestnut hair
On your forehead broad and fair,
                    Marguerite.

Ah, your voice is soft and low,
                    Marguerite,
But it thrills me thro' and thro',
                    Marguerite,
Like the cooing of a dove
Speaking to its mate of love,
                    Marguerite.

Your eyes are wells of truth,
                    Marguerite,
And what they say, in sooth,
                    Is so sweet,
That my heart goes out to meet you,
And with tenderest love doth greet you,
                    Marguerite.

The bloom upon your cheek,
                              Ah, my sweet,
Nestles in the rose heart deep,
                              Marguerite.
There 's a dimple in your chin
That my heart just fits within,
                              Ma petite.

From the ring upon your hand,
                              Marguerite,
To the dainty little slippers
                              On your feet,
And the chestnut crown above them,
I love them all—I love them,
                              Marguerite.

When from off your winsome face,
                              Marguerite,
Ruthless time has torn youth's grace,
                              Marguerite,
Still within my bosom's core,
Love will live for evermore,
                              Marguerite.

5:30 a. m.

Oh that proverbial early bird,
 —The one that caught the worm—
I would that I had never heard
Of that proverbial early bird!
A pious fraud, a snare absurd,
 I boldly do affirm,
Was that proverbial early bird—
 The one that caught the worm.

ENVOI.

And Prince, the *worm*—
He also rose betimes,
And yet, methinks his was a cruel fate.
Would it not seem the moral of the tale
Were this—'Twere best to lie full *late?*

"ICH liebe dich," was all he said.
And why I should have blushed so red,
  I can not say—I do not know;
  The words could not have moved me so—
It must have been his look instead.

But why should I have hung my head,
And really almost felt afraid,
  When what he meant I did not know,
        "Ich liebe dich"?

"Three German words" they were, he said.
"Teach me the meaning? No, instead
  The words themselves he'd teach, and so
  The meaning soon enough I'd know."
And soon my faltering lips he led
To say the words himself had said—
        "Ich liebe dich."

YOUTH and love and a summer day —
    What fairer gifts could the gods bestow ?
Ah, could the golden time but stay,
    Of youth and love and a summer day !

If the grass would cover the brown old ground,
And the sun would shine the whole year 'round,
If youth lent wings to the dancing breeze,
And love gave lips to the whispering trees,
If youth and love would never leave us,
No fairer gifts the gods could give us !

THE sun kissed the clover,
    Each blossom blushed red—
For kisses bring blushes,
    'Tis said.

Oh young maids are charming,
    And ribbons are blue,
And boys are still saucy
    At blithe twenty-two.

The sun kissed the clover—
    Sweet Nancy blushed too.
Now who kissed sweet Nancy
    I wonder—don't you?

La Glu.

BRITTANY FOLK SONG.

ONCE upon a time there was a poor boy.
—Oulie oulai oulie oula—
Once upon a time there was a poor boy
Who loved one
Who loved him not.

She said to him "bring me to-day,"
—Oulie oulai oulie oula—
She said to him "bring me to-day
The heart of thy mother
For my dog."

He goes to his home and his mother kills.
—Oulie oulai oulie oula—
He goes to his home and his mother kills,
Seizes the heart
And runs away.

In running away down he falls.
—Oulie oulai oulie oula—
In running away down he falls,
And the heart
Rolls on the ground.

As it rolls it speaks to him.
—Oulie oulai oulie oula—
As it rolls it speaks to him—
Listen thou
To what it says.

As it rolls it weeping says,
—Oulie oulai oulie oula—
As it rolls it weeping says,
"Art thou hurt
My poor child?"

MON Ami fierce and tender,
　　What mischief hast thou planned?
What would'st thou I should render,
Mon Ami fierce and tender?
The gods must well defend her
　　Who would thy siege withstand!
Mon Ami fierce and tender,
　　What mischief hast thou planned?

Ah food for sighs and laughter
　　Thy "game" is, mon Ami.
And what will follow after
Is food for sighs and laughter!
Thy voice is even softer—
"He flirts unconsciously—"
Ah food for sighs and laughter,
　　Thy "game" is, mon Ami.

BALLAD

OF

The Reformed Pirate.

A STUDY IN TRANSMIGRATION

—

IN the far off Middle Ages,
　—When that was I have no notion—
Out upon the dreary ocean
　Roved a robber fierce and bold.
And, if we believe the story,
So particularly gory
Was this dark and dreadful villain,
　That the half has ne'er been told.

For he braved the raging billows,
And he feared not man nor demon.
He was quite an able seaman,
　And his craft was sure and fast.
Oh, he lived at quite a high rate,
Did this dark and dreadful pirate,
For his flag was black as midnight
　And he nailed it to the mast!

Thus for many a year he plundered,
Robbed and murdered, swore and thundered,
But at last the villain blundered,
  —Which was well, upon the whole.
So they made a little rope fast,
And they hung him from the topmast.
—It may strike you as peculiar ;
  But that pirate had a soul.

Had a soul above his station,
And in spite of his vocation,
He'd a liberal education,
  —Which is well, upon the whole.
And, besides his navigation,
Knew the doctrine of negation,
And about the transmigration
  Of his own piratic soul.

Ah, but hear the end pathetic—
For I know the sad possessor
Of the soul of this transgressor
  'Gainst the laws of God and man ;
Though the strange and curious history
Of the dark and dreadful mystery—
'Neath correctness of demeanor
  He will hide *it* if he can.

Now, instead of oaths piratic,
He writes verses enigmatic ;
Though he soothes his soul with triolets,
  He sometimes makes a slip.
But he leads a model life now,
And deals no more in strife now ;
He's the mildest mannered man now
  That ever scuttled ship.

He goes in for metaphysics,
And he's great at the poetics,
But, alas, he gets no solace
  From the jingle of his rhyme.
Though he laughs a mirthless laughter,
Yet the look that follows after
Is of rayless melancholy,
  For his *soul* is steeped in crime.

THE day seems filled with mad mirth,
The merry breezes start ;
There's sunshine on the glad earth,
There sunshine in my heart.

The day seems hardly sober,
There's gold on every tree ;
It brings the world October—
It brings my Love to me.

THOU'RT "Friendship's pledge," my pretty rose,
   And not a lover's token.
One scarce would guess, unless one knows,
   Thou'rt " Friendship's pledge," my pretty rose.
From that faint blush one would suppose
   There were sweet words unspoken.
Thou'rt " Friendship's pledge," my pretty rose,
   And not a lover's token?

MY heart a willing captive lies
In twisted chains of golden hair.
Grim warders twain two deep blue eyes;
—My heart a willing captive lies—
The prisoner who from fetters flies
Like mine, is found extremely rare.
My heart a *willing* captive lies
In twisted chains of golden hair.

TRANSLATIONS FROM HEINE.

I CALLED the Devil, and he came.
  With wonderment his form I scan ;
  He is not ugly, is not lame,
    He is a dear and charming man
Just in the prime of life, and so
Quite up in the ways of the world, you know.
Talking of Church and State with tact—
A bit of a diplomat, in fact.
No wonder he 's pale, and hollow his eyes,
Since Sanscrit and Hegel his studies comprise.
His favorite poet is still Fouque,
But with the critics he will not bother ;
He has turned that over to his grandmother,
His dear grandmother, Hecate.
To my legal efforts he gave his praise,
Said he 'd thought of the law in his younger days.
He vowed my acquaintance an honor and credit,
And bowed with an infinite grace as he said it.
Then he asked if the Spanish Embassador
Had not presented us one to the other ?
I looked with more care than I had before,
And found in him my friend and brother.

AH, if thou wert my wedded wife,
    Much envied would 'st thou be ;
For thou should 'st live for pure pastime,
    And fare right joyously.

Thy scoldings and thy stormings
    I 'd suffer patiently ;
But if thou should 'st not praise my songs,
    Then would I part from thee.

HE is a god who first time loves,
　　Tho' he may love in vain ;
But by the gods he is a fool
　　Who hapless loves again.

And such a fool am I—once more
　　Of hopeless love I sigh.
Sun, moon, and stars, they laugh at me,
　　And I laugh, too—and die.

THOU'RT like a lovely flower,
   So pure and fair thou art,
And when I look upon thee
   Strange sadness fills my heart.

It seems to me that I should lay
   My hands upon thy brow,
And pray that God will keep thee
   As pure and fair as now.